There Are No Polar Bears Here!

by Catherine Simpson

Illustrated by Joanne Snook

Tuckamore Books
a **Creative Publishers** imprint
St. John's, Newfoundland
1995

One Saturday in May, Kerry was picking partridgeberries on the hill above the Cove. Her bucket was almost full when she remembered that the sweetest ones grew up behind Puzzle Rock.

She was bending over, getting her fingers red with squashy berries when she heard a snuffle and a whuffle. She looked up. There, on the slope above her, stood a bear. A polar bear. Jumpins!

Kerry had learned about bears in school. She didn't panic. She pushed her bucket of berries towards the bear and backed away slowly. The bear shuffled forward and started to munch.

Kerry ran back to the cove. The first person she saw was Uncle Ron, fixing his fence.

"I saw a polar bear!" she said.

"Impossible, my duckie. There are no polar bears here," he said.

"Yes, there are," said Kerry. "I saw one. I know a bear when I see one."

Kerry ran on until she spotted
Aunt Jean, hanging clothes.

"I saw a polar bear!" she said.

"Impossible, my trout. There
are no polar bears here," she answered.

"Yes, there are," said Kerry. "I saw one. I know a bear
when I see one."

Kerry was almost home when she met
Mr. Sharpe, loading his truck.

"I saw a polar bear!" she said.

"Impossible, my maid. There are no polar bears here," he said.

"Yes, there are," said Kerry. "I saw one. I know a bear when I see one."

Nobody would believe her.

Next day, Kerry was sweeping the kitchen. When she opened the back porch door, there on the steps stood the polar bear, wiggling his big black nose. Jumpins!

Kerry didn't panic. She banged on the garbage can with the broomstick and made a deafening cacophony. The bear turned and scurried back up over the hil

"Kerry, what's the fuss?" called her mother, running from the garden.

"Kerry, what's the hullabaloo?" called her father, running from his workshop.

"Kerry, what's the racket?" called her brother, running from his video game.

"I just drove away the polar bear," Kerry said. "He was coming up the back steps."

"Kerry, Kerry, Kerry," they said. " That's impossible. There are no polar bears here."

"Yes, there are," said Kerry. "I saw one. I know a bear when I see one." Nobody would believe her.

Next morning, Kerry
took a shortcut to school
through a patch of woods where
hummocks of leftover snow still lay hard
and white in the shady places. Ahead of her
on the path, a particularly large hummock
was hulking. It was no snowdrift. Jumpins!

She didn't panic. She spoke softly and unwrapped her lunch. "Hello again, bear. Have my partridgeberry bun." She tossed it out into the woods and the bear shuffled after it, snuffling and whuffling.

At school, Kerry told her news.

"Are you sure it wasn't a sheep?" asked Thomas.

"Are you sure it wasn't a sheepdog?" asked Isabel.

"Are you sure it wasn't an iceberg?" asked Tracey.

"It must have been a figment of your imagination," said Ms. Primmer.

Kerry rolled her eyes and sighed. "It was a bear. I know a bear when I see one."

Nobody would believe her.

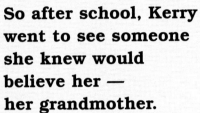

So after school, Kerry went to see someone she knew would believe her — her grandmother.

"I saw a polar bear," she said.

"Where?" asked her grandmother.

"Up by Puzzle Rock, on our back steps, and on the shortcut. But nobody will believe me."

"Why not?" asked her grandmother.

"They think I'm making it up. They say there are no polar bears here."

"Maybe they need to see it with their own eyes," her grandmother said.

She gave Kerry a tin of partridgeberry squares. "These are for your mother, and this big one is for you. See you at the bean supper tonight."

On her way home, Kerry climbed up to Puzzle Rock. She'd forgotten about the bean supper. Everyone in the Cove would be there. If only the bear could be   there too! But how could she get him to go there?

If she were a detective, she could track him down and turn him in.

If she were a cowboy, she could go out and round him up.

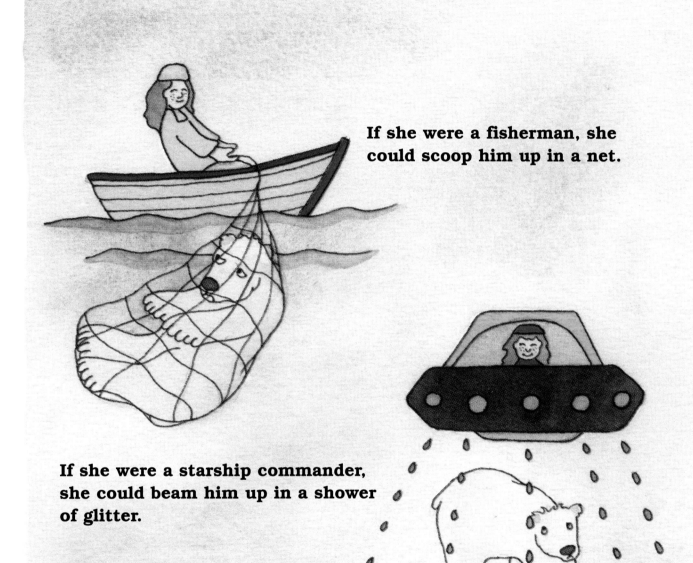

If she were a fisherman, she could scoop him up in a net.

If she were a starship commander, she could beam him up in a shower of glitter.

Kerry sighed. It was useless. There was no way to get the bear to the bean supper, unless . . . Bingo! She had an idea.

She rummaged in her schoolbag, took out a pencil and paper, and printed in large letters:

Dear Bear
plese come to the Bean supper tonigte so that evryone will see you.
your frind
Kerry

She read the invitation out loud, just in case the bear might be lurking nearby. Then she placed it beside Puzzle Rock and anchored it with a partridgeberry square.

That evening everyone in the Cove went to the bean supper in the community hall. Kerry's whole family went, along with her grandfather and grandmother. Uncle Ron and Aunt Jean and Mr. Sharpe went with their fathers and mothers and sons and daughters, too. So did Ms. Primmer and all the kids from school and their brothers and sisters and fathers and mothers and grandfathers and grandmothers and cousins and even their second cousins once removed.

Everyone sat down and feasted on pork and beans baked in molasses. For dessert, there was partridgeberry pudding. But Kerry couldn't touch a bite. Her stomach was full of butterflies. Would he or wouldn't he show up?

The hall got hotter and hotter. People ate and ate and ate. Soon, all the grownups were leaning back with red faces, sipping their tea and fanning themselves with their napkins. Some of the older folks were snoring and most of the babies were sound asleep.

Someone groaned, "My Blessed, how hot it is! Open the door before we all cook!"

Uncle Ron braced the door open. A cool breeze drifted in, bringing sounds from outside, a car going by, dogs barking. Suddenly, Kerry sat bolt upright. Her heart flipped head over heels. What was that sound?

It was a snuffle.

Then she heard another sound, closer.
It was a whuffle.

Then came a shuffle, shuffle, shuffle.

And right through the open door came a wiggly black nose, followed by a big white polar bear body. Jumpins!

Kerry wanted to run and kiss him, but she knew he wouldn't appreciate that, so she took her pudding and put it on the floor in front of him. He munched gratefully.

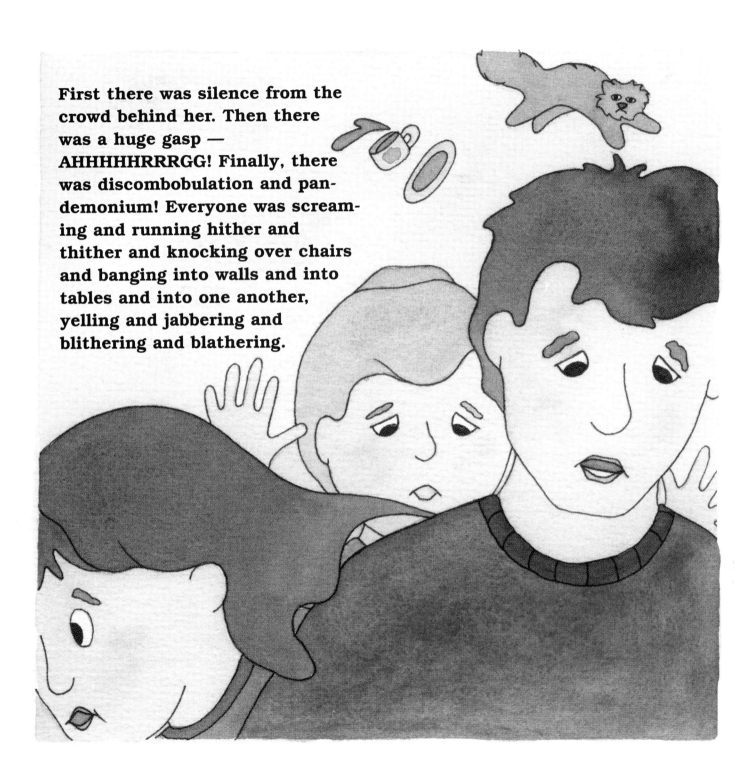

First there was silence from the crowd behind her. Then there was a huge gasp — AHHHHHRRRGG! Finally, there was discombobulation and pandemonium! Everyone was screaming and running hither and thither and knocking over chairs and banging into walls and into tables and into one another, yelling and jabbering and blithering and blathering.

"Jumpins! Help! A polar bear! We thought she was makin' it all up! Call the cops! Call the wildlife! Call the fire department!"

Kerry stood smiling at the panic. Now, at last, everyone believed her. She turned to thank the bear, but—he was gone. Vanished. Just like that!

She ran outside.
The setting sun was turning
everything in the Cove pink.
Kerry saw houses, lines of
wash, hummocks of old snow,
sheep on the hills, ice in the
harbour. But where was the bear?

"There you are!" she whispered.

There he was, just a speck far out on the
salt water, swimming back to the ice edge,
back to the North. At least, she thought it was
the bear. It might have been a piece of ice.

But probably not. After all,
Kerry knows a bear when she sees one.

*In memory of
my mother*

 Catherine Simpson grew up in Grand Falls, Newfoundland, and graduated from Memorial University. Working full-time as a writer and needlework designer, she finds endless inspiration in the culture, history, and natural environment of Newfoundland.She lives with her husband Jerry, son William, and dog Fergus on the northeast coast, where the spring ice really does bring polar bears ashore.

 Joanne Snook is a native Newfoundlander, and a graduate of Memorial University's School of Fine Arts in Corner Brook,Newfoundland. She has always admired the charm of the province's rural communities, and this is often reflected through her watercolour paintings. An artist for several years, this is the first children's book she has illustrated. She currently resides in St. John's.

© 1995, Catherine Simpson
Appreciation is expressed to *The Canada Council* for publication assistance.

The publisher acknowledges the financial contribution of the *Department of Tourism and Culture, Government of Newfoundland and Labrador,* which has helped make this publication possible.

Illustrations © 1995, Joanne Snook

Printed on acid-free paper

A Tuckamore Books imprint

Published by
CREATIVE BOOK PUBLISHING A DIVISION OF 10366 NEWFOUNDLAND LIMITED
A ROBINSON-BLACKMORE PRINTING & PUBLISHING ASSOCIATED COMPANY
P.O. Box 8660, St. John's, Newfoundland A1B 3T7

Printed in Canada by:
ROBINSON-BLACKMORE PRINTING & PUBLISHING

Canadian Cataloguing in Publication Data

Simpson, Catherine, 1953–

There are no polar bears here!

ISBN 1-895387-55-8

I. Snook, Joanne.   II. Title.

PS8587.I45T54 1995   jC813'.54   C95-950156-8 PZ7.S46Th 1995

Tuckamore Books
a **Creative Publishers** imprint